The Copper Tree

Words by Hilary Robinson

www.hilaryrobinson.co.uk

Pictures by Mandy Stanley

www.mandystanley.com

STRAUSS HOUSE PRODUCTIONS

Lumby Grange, Lumby, South Milford, North Yorkshire, LS25 5JA

www.thecoppertree.org

First published in Great Britain 2012

Text copyright © Hilary Robinson 2012

Illustrations copyright © Mandy Stanley 2012

Hilary Robinson and Mandy Stanley have asserted their rights

to be identified as the author and illustrator of this work under

The Copyright, Designs and Patents Act, 1988

British Library Cataloguing in Publication Data

A catalogue record for this book is available from the British Library

All rights reserved. ISBN 978-0-9571245-0-9

Printed in the UK

The Copper Tree

For Caroline
HR

For Dad
MS

Hilary Robinson & Mandy Stanley

STRAUSS HOUSE
PRODUCTIONS

When our teacher, Miss Evans, didn't come to school, Mr Banks asked us all to sit on the mat. We sang her favourite song All Things Bright and Beautiful.

Mr Banks said Miss Evans wasn't well but would try and pop in to see us from time to time.

We all made her a giant Get Well Soon card. I drew a bear with a plaster on its knee because Miss Evans put one on my knee once.

Alfie Tate rubbed out his name sixteen times because he kept making mistakes and there was nearly a hole in the page but Mr Banks said, 'not to worry, Miss Evans would understand.'

Miss Evans sent us a letter to say our card had really cheered her up. She said she would come and see our play which was Jack and the Beanstalk.

We only had one week to get it ready. Alfie Tate wanted to be the giant and he wasn't so there was fuss all the time.

When Miss Evans came to school she wore a sparkly scarf because she didn't have any hair. She was sitting in a wheelchair because she said she sometimes felt a bit wobbly. She smiled all the time.

Miss Evans was going to come to our Sports Day but she wasn't well enough. We thought it was a shame because Alfie Tate's dog did something amazing!

Dear Miss Evans

You'll never guess what happened at Sports Day! Do you remember Alfie Tate telling us he got his dog from a rescue centre and he had a sore leg and he'd called him Rocket? Well when Alfie wasn't looking Rocket ran off and won the three legged race!

Mr Banks tied a medal on his collar.

I was sad that I didn't see you but Mr Banks said you probably didn't feel up to it at the moment.

We had ice creams after the races but they melted a bit in the sun.
Love from Olivia x

Miss Evans wrote back with shaky writing to say
my letter and picture had really cheered her up.

A few days later Mr Banks said he had some sad news. Miss Evans had died. He said that even though there were times when she had suffered she wasn't in any pain at all when she died. I felt like crying and Mr Banks said it was okay to cry if we felt like it because sometimes crying helped us to feel a bit better. He said we might feel cross sometimes and that was okay too.

He played All Things Bright and Beautiful on the piano while we sat quietly.

Mr Banks said that if we felt sad then we could talk to him if we liked,
or to someone else who loves us, because sometimes talking to someone
could help us feel a bit better.

He said we might feel happy on some days and sad
on others but, in time, we would begin to feel better.

Mr Banks said we were going to think of ways to remember Miss Evans. Over the next few weeks we all thought about her and what she had taught us.

Hana said she taught her to share things like coloured pencils.

Jake said she taught him to grow tomatoes so he'd think of her every time he planted a pip.

Alfie Tate said she taught him how important it was to say sorry as he was always having to go to her desk for being naughty.

sorry !

Alfie said Miss Evans taught him about seasons as well.
They'd both jumped up and down in the playground
when he saw the first swallows of summer.

Alfie Tate has a bat box in his garden.
He knows a lot about bats.

We wrote our thoughts on remember notes.
Alfie Tate drew his. Mr Banks said that our
thoughts would be inscribed on leaves
made out of copper.

Our Caretaker, Stan, put up a tree made of copper wire in the entrance hall.

We invited Miss Evans's family in to to see what we had done.

Mr Banks said that even though Miss Evans wasn't here anymore she had left us with lots of memories and skills that we would keep for ever. We took it in turns to say our names and read out what was on our copper leaves. Alfie Tate showed us a picture of a bird on his. Then we hung them on the tree and do you know what...

they jingled like wind charms and they looked bright and beautiful in the sunbeams which was amazing, really, because...

love

reading stories

telling jokes

action songs

baking

looking after animals

making things

writing

...we all said that's just what Miss Evans was like.

Holly   Rupal   Olivia   Alfie

Jake   Erika   Hana   Barnie

Henry

www.strausshouseproductions.com

www.thecoppertree.org